THREAT TO THE LEATHERBACK TURTLE

Bonnie Hinman

P.O. Box 196
Hockessin, Delaware 19707
Visit us on the web: www.mitchelllane.com
Comments? email us: mitchelllane@mitchelllane.com

Mitchell Lane
PUBLISHERS

Printing   1   2   3   4   5   6   7   8   9

A Robbie Reader/On the Verge of Extinction: Crisis in the Environment

Library of Congress Cataloging-in-Publication Data
Hinman, Bonnie.
Threat to the leatherback turtle / by Bonnie Hinman.
    p. cm. — (On the verge of extinction. Crisis in the environment)
"A Robbie Reader."
Includes bibliographical references and index.
ISBN 978-1-58415-690-1 (library bound : alk. paper)
1. Leatherback turtle—Juvenile literature. 2. Endangered species—Juvenile literature. I. Title.
QL666.C546H56 2009
333.95'79289—dc22

                                                                                    2008020914

ABOUT THE AUTHOR: Bonnie Hinman grew up on a farm and has been fascinated by animals all her life. She loves to read about the ocean and its creatures. She graduated from Missouri State University and is the author of twenty books for young readers. She lives in Southwest Missouri with her husband, Bill, near her children and three grandsons.

PHOTO CREDITS: Cover, p. 1—Amigos de Las Baulas; p. 1 (inset)—University of Oregon; p. 4—AP Photo/Daytona Beach News-Journal, Brian Myrick; p. 7—KIDO Ecological Research Station; p. 8—Peabody Museum of Natural History; p. 10—Carly Peterson; p. 12—The Archie Carr National Wildlife Refuge; p. 13—Earth Hope Network; p. 14—NOAA; p. 15—Jupiterimages; p. 16—The New Naturalist; p. 19 (left)—Jupiterimages; p. 19 (right)—John Carroll; p. 20—AP Photo/New England Aquarium; p. 21—Rob Kahala; p. 22—World Wildlife Fund, NJ. Tangkepayung; p. 24—NOAA; p. 25—Great Barrier Reef Marine Park Authority; p. 26—Amy Prinsloo; p. 27—Stacy Kubis; p. 28—AP Photo/The St. Petersburg Times, John Pendygraft; Interior background—Sharon Beck.

PLB

TABLE OF CONTENTS

Words in **bold** type can be found in the glossary.

A leatherback turtle laying eggs. Once a female leatherback is settled in her sandy pit and begins to lay eggs, she seems to go into a trance. Nothing scares or interrupts her as she does her job. Scientists and volunteers use this time to measure and tag her. People are allowed to touch her tough skin. They often are concerned because the turtle seems to be crying. A leatherback's tears are her body's way of getting rid of salt. They don't mean that she is sad or scared.

A MOTHER TURTLE

A large dark shape appears in the waves near a Costa Rican beach and heads steadily toward the shore. It is night, but in minutes a watcher can see that the shape is a sea turtle. The waves help the turtle swim, and it is cast onto the beach. The turtle **trudges** up the beach away from the water.

This barrel-shaped reptile is a leatherback, one of seven different kinds of sea turtles that live in the world's oceans. All sea turtles are considered **endangered** (en-DAYN-jerd), or at risk of becoming **extinct**. The leatherback is seriously endangered.

This leatherback has come to the beach to lay her eggs. She moves rather quickly for her size—she weighs more than 1,500 pounds—but pulling herself through sand is hard, and she must stop to rest. She uses her winglike front flippers to do most of the work, while her much smaller back flippers help steer her huge body. She climbs a slight incline toward the dark rain forest shadows ahead.

At the rain forest's edge she pauses to rest, then turns to her main task. Sand flies as she uses her powerful front flippers to chop into the ground, making a pit for her body. When the pit is large enough, she settles into it and uses her rear flippers to dig a smaller hole under her tail.

When the depth and shape of the hole suit her, she lays sixty to eighty eggs. They drop in, one by one. Then she sweeps sand into the hole with her rear flippers. She gently pats the sand after each scoop until the nest is covered. Then she uses her front flippers to throw huge scoops of sand over the entire egg-laying area.

When a leatherback female has laid most of her eggs, she lays about two dozen more smaller eggs. These are called "false eggs" because they contain no yolk to feed a developing hatchling. Scientists are not sure, but the extra eggs may provide air space at the top of the nest or some other protection for the developing hatchlings.

She twists and turns to throw sand until it is impossible to see the nest's location. When she stops her thrashing, she heads to the ocean. Soon she reaches the water's edge and lets the waves lift her back into the dark sea.

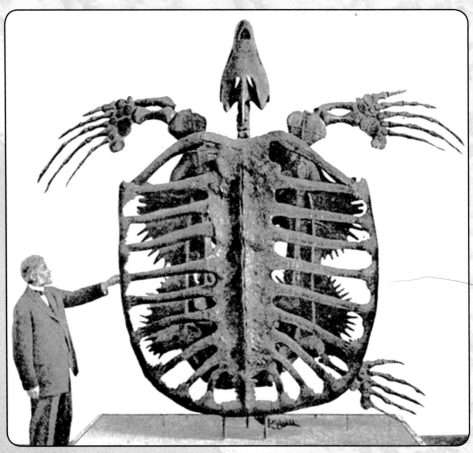

Archelon (AR-keh-lon) fossil, in Yale's Peabody Museum of Natural History, discovered in 1895. Archelon was the biggest sea turtle that ever lived. Fossil discoveries show that it weighed about 6,000 pounds and was 15 feet long, nose to tail. Its head was three feet long and had a huge beak. This ancient turtle was related to modern sea turtles, but that family of turtles became extinct.

AN ANCIENT REPTILE

The leatherback is one of the seven kinds of sea turtles that don't have a hard shell. It is the largest of the sea turtles. Its top shell, called a **carapace** (KAYR-uh-pis), can be as long as six feet. The turtle gets its name because of the tough, leathery skin that covers its carapace.

Under the skin are thousands of tiny bones that strengthen its back and cover a thick layer of fat. Scientists sometimes call the turtle the last of the dinosaurs because of its huge size—and because its ancestors lived at the same time as dinosaurs.

A leatherback is a **pelagic** (pih-LAA-jik) turtle, since it spends most of its life

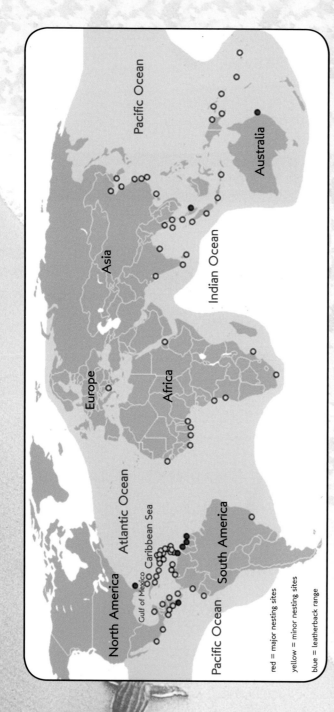

Leatherbacks may migrate (MY-grayt) thousands of miles and still return to nest on the same beach every two or three years. Scientists think that one reason the turtles know where they are has to do with Earth's magnetic fields. Sea turtles and several other species have tiny magnetite crystals in their brains. It appears that these crystals act like a compass that helps them navigate (NAA-vih-gayt) the oceans to find feeding and nesting areas.

Within the map:

Pacific Ocean

Australia

Asia

Indian Ocean

Europe

Africa

Atlantic Ocean

North America

Gulf of Mexico
Caribbean Sea

South America

Pacific Ocean

red = major nesting sites

yellow = minor nesting sites

blue = leatherback range

swimming and feeding far out to sea. Its favorite food is jellyfish, and it may swim thousands of miles to find the best feeding places. It is a fast swimmer and can dive as deep as 4,000 feet, which is deeper than any other reptile.

Leatherbacks swim far north and south in the world's oceans as they **migrate** to different feeding grounds. Atlantic leatherbacks often swim north to feed on jellyfish near Newfoundland in Canada. They also go as far south as South Africa.

Pacific leatherbacks feed and nest from California and Mexico to China, Indonesia, and Australia. All leatherbacks return to warmer waters for mating and egg-laying. Female leatherbacks return to the same area where they hatched to lay their own eggs.

Leatherbacks usually lay eggs every two or three years. When they return to the nesting beaches, they lay clutches, or groups, of eggs every ten days or so up to seven times before they head back out to the open

When a leatherback female heads for the sea after laying her eggs, her tracks look like a vehicle has driven on the beach. The female pulls herself forward with her front flippers to the water's edge. It takes her only a few minutes to get down the beach because she is eager to get back to the sea.

Leatherback eggs are about the size of tennis balls and aren't hard like birds' eggs. They feel like leather or parchment. A hatchling can break out of its shell in a few hours but often rests for a day or two before starting to climb up and out of its sandy nest.

sea. They do not protect their eggs, nor do they return to raise their babies.

In 45 to 70 days, the eggs stir in their sandy nest. The hatchlings use a small tooth on their beak to tear at the rubbery shell. Soon there will be several hatchlings scrambling to the beach surface. It can be two days before the turtles pop into the fresh air. With only the bright water to guide them, they race across the open beach to reach the sea. After several days of furious paddling, the hatchlings seem to disappear.

The sex of a hatchling is determined by the temperature of the sand surrounding the nest. If the sand temperature is 85 degrees Fahrenheit, the hatchlings will be a mix of males and females. If the temperature is above 85 degrees, most of the turtles will be female. If it is below 85 degrees, most of them will be male.

Young leatherbacks might hide from predators in floating seaweed. Not only does it provide camouflage, but it is also a source of food.

Scientists often call the first few years of a leatherback's life "the lost years," because where the turtles live during this time is a mystery. They may live in huge seaweed mats that drift on the ocean. They aren't seen again until they are much bigger, when they begin to wander the world's oceans.

Leatherback turtles are the largest of the sea turtles, at four to eight feet in length and 500 to 2,000 pounds in weight. The next largest sea turtles are green turtles and loggerhead turtles, who can grow to about four feet long and weigh around 450 pounds.

LEATHERBACK ENEMIES

Trouble starts early for leatherbacks. Dogs, raccoons, and people steal eggs from the nests. Leatherback meat isn't very good to eat, but eggs are considered a **delicacy** (DEH-lik-kuh-see) in some countries. Once hatched, the tiny turtles are targets for ghost crabs, pelicans, and gulls as they sprint to the sea.

Once they reach the ocean, sharks and octopuses and other sea creatures grab the two-ounce turtles as they paddle to reach a hiding place in seaweed. Very few hatchlings survive to become adults.

Once a leatherback grows too big to be gulped down by a fish or octopus, humans become its greatest enemy. **Commercial** (kuh-MUR-shul) fishermen don't catch the big turtles on purpose, but they do catch them by accident. This accidental catching is one of the reasons that leatherback turtles are endangered.

Shrimp boats drag long nets behind them. The nets catch shrimp and, without aiming to, other fish and turtles. Gill nets are large floating mesh nets that entangle fish and other creatures as they swim. A leatherback can hold its breath underwater for around 45 minutes but will drown eventually. Longline fishing lines may stretch for miles. They dangle curtains of thousands of hooks to catch swordfish, tuna, and other big fish. Leatherbacks can get tangled and drown or be left with hooks in their mouths or stomachs.

Pollution (puh-LOO-shun) in the ocean also causes turtle deaths. Oil and other chemicals have spilled into the seas for many years. All kinds of **debris** (deh-BREE) floats

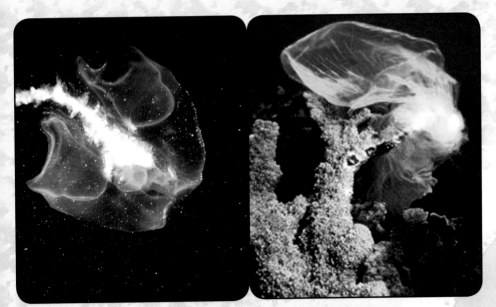

It is easy to see how leatherbacks might mistake a plastic bag (right) for a jellyfish (left). Garbage in the ocean is a threat to turtles of all kinds, but plastic is especially dangerous. It can block a turtle's airways or intestines and kill it.

in the water, especially near the coasts. Plastic products are the worst because they don't **dissolve** (dih-ZOLV). Floating plastic bags look like jellyfish to a turtle, but swallowing one can kill a turtle of any size.

Constructing buildings near nesting beaches is another way humans cause dangers for leatherbacks. Sometimes the beaches themselves are destroyed, but more often the lighting is what causes the problem. Turtles use levels of light to help find where to nest. Too much light can confuse the females and cause them to nest below the high-tide line. Hatchlings use the natural

This leatherback was brought to the New England Aquarium in Boston after being found on a nearby beach where it had crawled ashore two days in a row. It is very rare for leatherbacks to come ashore except for laying eggs. Aquarium scientists said that the turtle was extremely ill.

A tiny hatchling briefly loses its way to the ocean. Turtles are least attracted to yellow or red lights, so using these colors for shore lighting is a good way to keep females and hatchlings from becoming confused.

brightness of the sea at night to find their way to the water. Shore lights confuse them, allowing more time for predators to catch them on land.

There are many threats to leatherbacks, but there are also many people working hard to save them.

Scientists placed a three-part harness on a nesting female while she was laying eggs. The satellite transmitter rests on her back and is designed to fall off in about a year when the batteries run out. This method is expensive but it offers a way to locate a migrating leatherback anywhere in the world at any time. Scientists also use metal flipper tags and implanted microchips to track leatherbacks and other sea turtles.

SAVING LEATHERBACKS

Efforts to protect leatherbacks begin on beaches at night. Scientists and volunteers **patrol** (puh-TROHL) during the yearly nesting times. When a nesting leatherback is spotted, she is watched until she safely lays her eggs. Some females are fitted with satellite transmitters.

After the female has gone back to the ocean, the nest may be marked to allow it to be guarded. Sometimes the eggs will be moved to a safer area until they hatch. Patrolling continues through hatching time. Hatchlings need to dash quickly from the nest to the ocean, so it is important to keep the lights off near nesting beaches.

Oceanside **communities** (kuh-MYOO-nih-tees) near leatherback nesting beaches in Florida have laws that require residents to turn off or shield their outdoor lights during nesting season. Some towns hire inspectors to make sure that people obey these laws.

Several countries have made laws to help sea turtles avoid the dangers they face from commercial fishing. Shrimp boats off United States coasts have to put turtle

A loggerhead turtle escapes from a shrimp net through a turtle excluder device (TED). There are different kinds of TEDs, but all have a trap door that lets the turtle swim out of the net before it enters the far end where shrimp or other fish collect.

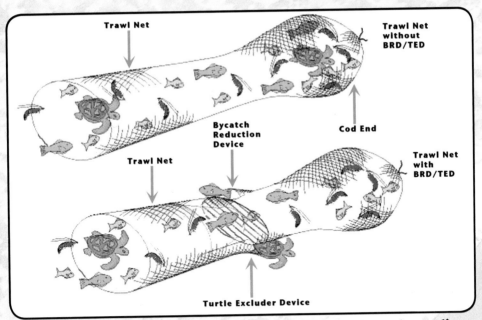

Trawl Net

Trawl Net without BRD/TED

Bycatch Reduction Device

Cod End

Trawl Net

Trawl Net with BRD/TED

Turtle Excluder Device

Fishermen have resisted using TEDs, but several studies suggest that using them can save as many as half of the turtles caught in nets. BRDs (bycatch reduction devices) also allow other unwanted fish, such as cod, to escape.

excluder (ek-SKLOO-der) devices, called TEDs, in their nets. The TEDs are escape holes that let turtles get out but keep the shrimp in.

Gill nets have been banned off the Florida coasts, but they are still widely used near turtle nesting beaches in countries other than the United States. Experts say it is possible to use gill nets without hurting turtles, but the nets must be small and checked every hour. Fishermen say it would be expensive to use this method.

It's hard to make longline fishing less dangerous for turtles, but fishermen have been **experimenting** (ek-SPEHR-eh-men-ting) with round hooks and using bait that turtles don't like. The round hooks do less damage to a turtle if it gets snagged.

Pollution of the world's oceans is a big problem. The United States and other countries are making more and more laws to stop the flow of garbage into the seas, but obeying them takes time and cooperation from regular citizens.

Scientists have found many ways to help leatherbacks increase their numbers. They protect the eggs and hatchlings, tag and track

A shrimp trawler hauls in its catch. Before stricter laws were placed on trawlers, up to 80 percent of a boat's catch could be unwanted animals, including sea turtles.

George Shillinger helped found the Great Turtle Race. The first race took place from April 16 to 29, 2007. Sponsors paid for eleven female leatherbacks to be fitted with satellite transmitters while they nested on a Costa Rican beach on the Pacific Ocean. When the turtles headed to their feeding areas near the Galápagos Islands, they were tracked to see who got there first. The race raised over $225,000 to help with leatherback turtle conservation.

females, study leatherback migration, and educate young people about turtles.

Despite these efforts, leatherbacks in the Pacific Ocean are very seriously endangered, and their numbers decrease steadily year by

Marine trainer Coni Romano covers Anna, a leatherback turtle, with a damp towel to keep her wet and warm as she rests in the shallow water at Clearwater Marine Aquarium in Florida. Anna caught her left front flipper in a crab trap line, and it had to be removed. Human activities such as fishing remain the largest threat to leatherback turtles.

year. Atlantic leatherbacks are doing better. They are still endangered, but their numbers are steady and may be increasing a little. It's up to all of us to keep these huge yet graceful animals from becoming extinct.

Recycle Plastic
Plastic bags and containers from anywhere in the world might end up in the ocean. Learn how you can recycle plastic in your community. And PLEASE DON'T LITTER.

Adopt-A-Turtle
Visit the Caribbean Conservation Corporation web site at www.cccturtle.org to find out how you can contribute money and adopt a sea turtle. To raise money, you can ask a teacher or other adult if you can hold a yard sale or bake sale.

Track Leatherbacks
The TOPP (Tagging of Pacific Predators) program tracks several kinds of Pacific predators including leatherback turtles. The tracking information is compiled on the TOPP web site at www.topp.org. You can watch day by day as the tagged leatherbacks move from nesting beaches to feeding grounds.

Visit a Nesting Beach
Leatherback nesting beaches are close to both Disney World and Cape Canaveral in Florida. If you live near there or are going there for vacation, ask your parents if you can visit a nesting beach in person.

Learn More
Read all you can about leatherbacks and other sea turtles. There are several books listed in the next section that can get you started. Also listed are web sites with information about leatherbacks.

Books

Arnosky, Jim. *All About Turtles.* New York: Scholastic Press, 2000.

Cerullo, Mary. *Sea Turtles: Ocean Nomads.* New York: Dutton Juvenile, 2003.

Guiberson, Brenda. *Into the Sea.* New York: Henry Holt and Co., 2000.

Hickman, Pamela. *Turtle Rescue: Changing the Future for Endangered Wildlife.* Richmond Hill, Ontario: Firefly Books, 2005.

Johnston, Marianne. *Sea Turtles, Past and Present.* New York: Powerkids Press, 2000.

Kalman, Bobbie. *The Life Cycle of a Sea Turtle.* New York: Crabtree Publishing Co., 2002.

Lasky, Kathryn. *Interrupted Journey: Saving Endangered Sea Turtles.* Cambridge, Massachusetts: Candlewick Press, 2001.

Rhodes, Mary Jo. *Sea Turtles.* Danbury, Connecticut: Children's Press, 2005.

Theodorou, Rod. *Leatherback Sea Turtle.* Chicago: Heinemann Library, 2001.

Works Consulted

Butvill, David Brian. "Coast Guards: A U.S. Education Group Sends Students to a Costa Rican Beach to Help Protect Leatherback Turtles." *Current Science,* September 22, 2006, Vol. 92, Issue 2.

Carr, Archie. *So Excellent a Fishe: A Natural History of Sea Turtles.* New York: The Natural History Press, 1967.

Earthwatch. "Leatherbacks Bounce Back." *Earthwatch Institute Journal,* November 2006, Vol. 26, Issue 2.

Safina, Carl. *Voyage of the Turtle; In Pursuit of the Earth's Last Dinosaur.* New York: Henry Holt and Company, 2006.

Spotila, James R. *Sea Turtles: A Complete Guide to Their Biology, Behavior, and Conservation.* Baltimore and London: The Johns Hopkins University Press, 2004.

Starrett, Ashlee. "Tank Turtles Tell All." *Canadian Geographic,* March/April 2007, Vol. 127, Issue 2.

Vance, Eric. "Race for Survival." *Chronicle of Higher Education.* May 18, 2007, Vol. 53, Issue 37.

On the Internet

The Caribbean Conservation Corporation & Sea Turtle Survival League
http://www.cccturtle.org

Earthwatch Institute: Trinidad's Leatherback Sea Turtles
http://www.earthwatch.org/expeditions/sammy.html

The Leatherback Trust
http://www.leatherback.org

The Sea Turtle Restoration Project
http://www.seaturtles.org

carapace (KAYR-uh-pis)—The top shell of a turtle.

commercial (kuh-MUR-shul)—Having to do with business and making money.

communities (kuh-MYOO-nih-tees)—Areas where groups of people live close together.

debris (deh-BREE)—Small pieces of something that has broken down or died.

delicacy (DEH-lih-kuh-see)—A choice food not easily obtained.

dissolve (dih-ZOLV)—To mix with a liquid such as water and disappear.

endangered (en-DAYN-jerd)—At risk of becoming extinct.

experimenting (ek-SPEHR-eh-men-ting)—Testing to discover something unknown.

extinct (ek-STINKT)—No longer existing.

migrate (MY-grayt)—To move from one region to another, usually as a group.

navigate (NAA-vih-gayt)—To direct a course through water or air or on land.

patrol (puh-TROHL)—To guard by making regular trips along a certain path.

pelagic (pih-LAA-jik)—Of the open ocean.

pollution (puh-LOO-shun)—Chemicals and debris such as plastic that end up in the environment where it doesn't belong.

trudges (TRUD-jez)—Walks in a heavy way with much effort.

INDEX